"Praise for The Heart of Matter"

"...this is a wonderfully written and intriguing fantasy-driven story that seamlessly ties together its own mythology and touches on the life of an empath beautifully. I would definitely recommend anyone interested in either extraterrestrials, empaths and/or mediums, or the fantasy genre as a whole to read this incredible book, The Heart of Matter by Elizabeth Motley."

-Pacific Book Review"

The Heart of Matter

by:

E. M. Motley

ISBN
978-1-956529-44-9 (Paperback)
978-1-956529-43-2 (eBook)

For Cody and Jake,
and their bright futures

Table of Contents

Cameras 3

Big Brother...9

TV 15

Agenda..27

Extraterrestrials...35

Caged.. 41

Las Vegas or Lost Wages.......................................53

Attention Walmart Shoppers.................................61

Ascension and The Experiment 73

Life 85

Relief 95

Domestic Life 103

Predator and Clues 109

Encyclopedia 117

Gardening 121

Gaia 131

Hyrax 143

Fairies 151

Ability to Go Home 161

The Good Witch 173

Forgiveness 179

Inspirations and Recommendations: 185

About the Author 190

When they first looked at the large house, she thought the rental really nice but Bethany was focused on a house where the backyard bordered the bay. As fate would have it, the bay house wasn't available and with little time to find a new place, it looked like they would be moving into the large house. Bethany was trying to find out why she was so reluctant to move in.

Cameras

The house was open, a big beautiful two-story with a large grassy area across the street complete with a discreet redwood tree circle as it stood halved by a fence to delineate the perimeter of the park. The back patio had a deck with an open lattice structure overhead, completely enclosed with three gates. Bethany wasn't sure to keep in what? The rest of the backyard ground was covered with cement shaped liked pavers almost all the way to the fence line except for a winding strip of dirt.

Inside the house was a double-sided fireplace that opened to the family room / living room, and a floating walkway connecting the bedrooms on the second floor. It was a great house with lots of light from large windows, a high open ceiling, and a bay window in the kitchen like Bethany had always wanted. The final cue from the universe was the signature bushes that Bethany knew would be on her next home, and now their new home.

After years of living there, Bethany had found the similarities to the Jim Carrey movie eerily similar. The place felt like there were cameras installed everywhere. It seemed like remote devices tracked her and constantly monitored who she ran into, extending all the way to the nearby park, dictating which neighbors and dogs she encountered every day.

The sounds of the soccer games, field hockey practices, and parties in the park were offensive at first with their thunderous noise, and then just too loud for years. It sounded as if they lived on a soundstage and the games were being played in the backyard, the way the sound traveled from the park and then bounced off the houses directly behind them into their open windows and especially into the master bedroom. A street bordered their backyard, with parking alongside the fence line, and every latenight workaholic, partier, shift worker or night owl that drove down the street behind them sounded like they were revving the engine from inside the house, especially the half hour five to ten minute attempts it took to parallel park in an acceptable manner.

Does anyone really care how well they fucking park, much less at 2am in the morning? Most people rarely obey stop signs when they think no one is looking

Big Brother

As Bethany felt watched all the time, she couldn't be certain if it was the corrupted government acting as big brother or the extraterrestrials – the "bad" ones. It dawned on Bethany that she had never thought that perhaps she was being watched by the good ones – extraterrestrials that is. Ones that wanted to help her, and the ones she turned to for help constantly. What Bethany was thinking of, most people thought of as

Guardian Angels. Bethany wondered at the Angels existence and surmised that they were probably extraterrestrials wanting to make up for the free will experiment going horribly wrong? Or was it perfect?

Free will had gotten everyone into so much trouble. It had allowed the bad guys "aliens" who were currently in charge, to fuck up the planet and the people on it pretty badly. They (the bad guys) were soon to fail in a major way. Bethany knew that the extraterrestrials held technology far more advanced than most people could conceive. She hoped that it wasn't only the bad aliens watching her, that she wasn't being singled out and that everyone was being monitored. She already felt like enough of a freak.

A freak that really didn't give a shit what others thought about her but sometimes being the object of so much derision and scorn made her sad. Weary of knowing what others thought about her, but relieved to know that in the end it didn't matter.

Hearst Castle, San Simeon, CA

As an empath, Bethany could feel people's emotions, even if she incorrectly assumed that she was the cause or reason for those emotions. She tested ENFP on Meyers Briggs when she took it in the early 80's. Meyers Briggs said that her personality type was about five percent of the population. When Bethany was looking for resonance from humanity it seemed that percentage was closer to one-half of one percent.

And in the late 10's of the millennium, it felt like that fraction may need some more zeros after the decimal point as she seemed to be singular.

Bethany knew when people were lying, and she knew when people were annoyed with her when she lied. Bethany thought their annoyance odd since she sensed they weren't empaths, the only way that they could know she was lying was if they had seen the truth and knew otherwise— presumably on TV.

Bethany couldn't think of anything more lame than watching her life on TV. She was quite boring and nonsensical, and she knew people liked to make fun of her for her way of life. And Bethany knew she was being a hypocrite as she and her other watched Survivor, Amazing Race and Big Brother and she had made fun of the participants as well. At least the people participating knew that they were being filmed and had asked to be on the show. And got PAID for it.

There were a lot of times Bethany let people off the hook. Like when they knew things about her she hadn't told them, when they whispered names that they shouldn't know, when they admitted they knew where she'd been or what she'd done, revealing their knowledge of her life. Intimate details that would only be known to someone if they had been watching her.

She saw the drones as they monitored her, not even bothering to hide themselves, straight out in the open. And most times people were pretty obvious as they texted, videoed and relayed what she said to friends, videoed her in situations, with large cameras and massive lenses. She liked the people that were obvious about it, and then she could blast her ire and frustration straight at them and knew they could feel her rage. She hoped they had singe marks.

"WARNING"
THIS AREA IS UNDER
24 HOUR VIDEO
SURVEILLANCE

The "being watched" concept made ever more real by their actions. Her co-workers, neighbors and sometimes friends, obviously wanted to discuss whatever she had been up to and dissect what her thought process had been, get feedback from the directors and then tell her where she had gone wrong.

Bethany assumed people in general were getting their information via TV, but she couldn't understand why they would bother. Her life was so mundane. The only reason she figured anyone watched was because they were bored, waiting for their cameo on TV, have their five minutes of fame, or to make money.

Agenda

The way some of her co-workers pushed her to spill the tea, or just plain out irritate her until she reacted, was pretty consistent and mostly felt forced to Bethany. They (co-workers, neighbors, friends) always seemed to have seemed to have a checklist they needed to go through, or an itinerary of where they needed to take Bethany and what subject they needed to cover. Bethany wondered if they bet on what she would do next, if people gambled and made money watching her day to day on her conversations and actions.

At least Bethany would listen to the same song, ad infinitum. If they eavesdropped on her music choices while she had her headphones in, she knew she would be annoying them. This little rebellious act gave her a bit of cheer. She wondered if the if the producers or bad aliens used advanced technology to plant ideas in her head and see if they could get her to do things they made up. Perhaps Tomorrowland (Story by Damon Lindelof, Brad Bird, Jeff Jensen and Screenplay by Damon

Lindelof, Brad Bird, starring George Clooney) was today, and Earth was being fed daily doses of negative thoughts. The news did the job perfectly, especially with their never ending highlighting what was wrong with the world. Bethany felt like Athena in Tomorrowland, believing that Good was coming no matter what the news and reality showed her. Bethany certainly hoped that she didn't share the same fate as Athena to help people find the relief they were searching for.

She knew the aliens and probably the producers had the technology to radio thoughts along the airwaves. It was easy work to manipulate the humans. After tthe aliens made the most of the pinched-off cords connecting humans to their dynamic DNA, people were an easy target, easy to herd, children being led to the slaughter with every fear imaginable intertwined into daily life.

Most humans were kept in duress with the constant stress of providing for themselves and their families. Additionally, introduce toxins into their environment, into their food supply, and then contaminate the plants feeding them and the animals they feed upon.

It seems like a simple question. Why would any human put poison in their food? In their water? It seems more a question of who stands to gain from human frailty? Those controlling humans and their lives would.

An easy way to decrease the population when there were too many humans for the food supply and not enough of them dying. Why would any human put trust and faith in a government that was run by insurance and pharmaceutical companies telling them what is right and wrong instead of listening to their own gut?

Extraterrestrials

Bethany was pretty sure there were two different sets of aliens upon the Earth. Well actually, way more than that but for the sake of this train of thought, there were two kinds. The aliens that are poisoning humans, moving them around as slaves mining the planet, and the aliens that know the truth of our divinity and want us to know it too. Bethany felt sure that those extraterrestrials wanting our freedom had been muses to most, if not all of the uplifting literature, music, songs, speakers, movies and TV shows created. They constantly send messages of hope, faith, believing in your dreams, and overcoming all odds to find the beauty in life, treat all of our experiences with respect, and most of all – to have fun!

That was how the masters worked. Simple release of all judgement in every situation, and compassion for those of us lost in the experiment, as we treat it as more real than our true nature. Creators, divine sparks of God, here to express creatively and here to demonstrate that love truly conquers all.

And yet most of us addicted to feeling bad, impotent and sick.

Bethany believed that all of the empaths that came to Earth had a suicide pact if certain conditions were met as part of the Experiment. The instinct to go home was strong with Bethany. Since the age of six, she remembered that there was a place of all love, all the time, that felt the best, and living on Earth was certainly not cutting it, for sure.

Caged

Yesterday's evidence that Bethany was living a caged life as she was taking the dog for their evening walk. Bethany sensed more than saw intruders at the far end of the park as she saw the local soccer field / ad hoc neighborhood dog park come into view. She watched as two dogs jumped around on leash, while the owners stood still at a point near the edge of the farthest fence line surrounding the park, as a youth soccer game concluded.

Bethany intuited that the owners of the dogs were on a mission to interact with her and. Testing her theory, Bethany changed course, to walk her dog inside the park boundaries, versus the perimeter of the field where the interlopers waited. As soon as they saw that Bethany had changed her route and they would not intercept her at their current location, they cut through the middle of the park, intent on contact. Bethany saw this and still knowing that they meant to "run into her accidentally,"

Bethany double backed and headed back to the sidewalk outside of the park. If the intruders changed their tact and followed her now, they (and those directing them) knew it would blow up their efforts at remaining undercover.

As Bethany saw she had evaded them for the time being, she continued her walk, shelved the intrusion, and took her sweet time, cleaning up trash off the grass, sidewalk, and gutter as she went. The soccer players and their parents were clearing the field and getting in their cars as she passed them on the sidewalk.

Rounding the corner of the park on her usual path, Bethany realized the meddlers had not strayed from their mission and were standing at the corner waiting for her. She looked at them with knowing and they knew they had been caught. It had been too obvious, their insistence on being met by her, as Bethany had exhibited aberrant behavior to avoid them. The intruders held two small dogs (same approximate size as Bethany's dog) who had begun to growl and bark as they neared. Bethany's dog was equally aware of their dogs and hunched down in stalking mode.

Aliens, she surmised, disguised as young boys, and regardless of her obvious attempts to avoid them, they nervously waited for the encounter.

Bethany made a decision. If these beings really wanted to interact with the intent she assumed, to frighten and intimidate her, then so be it. The meddlers nervously looked on as Bethany and her dog approached, and they realized with certainty that she now MEANT to meet and greet them.

At about fifteen feet away, Bethany slowly leaned down, unleashed her dog, looked the other way, and let her dog have at it. She realized she didn't care if the dogs interacted and would let her dog express how they felt about being tracked like wild animals in a large enclosed pen. Bethany picked up some trash in her eyeline and then continued to search for trash while avoiding looking at the scene.

The interlopers held back their dogs, barking and shaking. While she sidestepped the outburst, Bethany heard the imposters dogs scream, and heard her dog barking and growling, and purposefully kept her eyes averted. As Bethany headed toward a trash can inside the park she finally turned her attention to the interaction to the interaction, only to see her dog very calmly walking away from the other dogs as they and the young boys were running away, and consequently away from her. And as she saw the last interloper head around the corner of the park, she saw the boy desperately trying to make eye contact, as if to imply he was sorry. Bethany stared back and waved a hand. The young boy wasn't sure if that was an acceptance of the apology but didn't wait to get confirmation and hightailed it around the corner out of sight.

Bethany had walked her dog around the park for many years. She used to know most if not all the dogs and people that walked regularly, and would greet new neighbors walking their dogs and get to know them until she was familiar with her neighborhood's canines and their owners.

She liked that so many people were out walking their dogs now. When she had first started walking her dog, there were very few other dogs and people out. Now, it was a veritable guarantee that she would she someone walking their dog whenever she was out.

Bethany was grateful for her internal alarm system. Especially when it alerted her and allowed her to tell when there was something off with the people she met or was directed to meet 'happenstance' at the park. Sometimes when on errands in town, Bethany liked to drive around and around in circles for all the cars tailing her to frustrate them and make them out themselves. Lol.

HAVE A LOT
TO SAY
ABOUT US.
THEY
THINK
THEY'VE
GOT US
FIGURED
OUT.
TIMES SQUARE
#aeri

Las Vegas or Lost Wages

Bethany assumed there had to be gambling on what she would do next. She felt that she was fed negative ideas about herself and others and that people would watch to see how she would react. When the people in charge didn't get the reaction they wanted, they would fuck with Bethany until they got a reaction...slow traffic to ten mph, flood empty streets with traffic, introduce nasty bitter people to interact with, and then have people step out into the street almost front of her car as she drove by to see if she was going to see them and stop.

Bethany had learned to check out when she was quite young as she had numerous encounters with men and women treating her like a sexual adult when she was ill equipped to deal with those situations at six or seven or et cetera years old. It caused her to put a massive wall around herself to try and block all the input she got as an empath because most people were pretty devious by nature. So in order to save her innocence she turned inward to stop the incoming messages from people by 'not seeing' them. 'I see you' being a specific reference to the James Cameron movie *Avatar* where the characters say 'I see you' to each other in a way that is a rarity on the surface of this planet but a lovely feel nonetheless.

Thus she mostly refrained from interaction with crowds and avoided any eye contact, and just watched the ground as she walked, paid attention to nature, the sky, anything but the multitudes of faces expressing feelings that came at her, sometimes like a gut punch. Bethany wondered why these strangers should aim destructive thoughts at her that felt very personal when they were supposed to be strangers in the crowd. So much derision directed towards her, she knew it was specific, sometimes a figurative slap in the face, obvious disgust at her, or ridicule for who she was being.

But sometimes when Bethany felt good and failed to keep her gaze down, there were kind faces in the crowd. Sometimes when Bethany looked up, she caught a smile, a door was opened, or she received a warm greeting. She guessed the producers had told the actors to treat her like she was invisible, nevertheless Bethany's kindness would elicit reciprocal feels in a few of the crowd and cause her great joy.

Kind of funny, because Bethany dreamed about being invisible, and the fun she would have. This was anything but fun. She knew they saw her and purposefully ignored her. She was so grateful to those who treated kindly.

Bethany was best one on one. That way she had only to deal with her emotions and those of one other person. When there was more than one person, situations became tricky to navigate as it became more difficult to detect which emotion was coming from which person and the honesty of the encounters became murky. Was there any truth to this situation or was it being carefully directed, and monitored? That was the principal question for Bethany every day of her life.

She had had them. Honest interactions.

Attention Walmart Shoppers

She guessed that the 'directors' asked the actors from time to time to vtake the longest amount of time possible to do any task as Bethany went about her day and ran her errands. Sometimes people took pity on Bethany and got on with it or redirected the conversation to something banal to give her a break.

Bethany thought the effort in their interactions obvious and contrived. She assumed most people went through with whatever they were asked to and/or agreed to, even if they felt silly to do so, to save face. Even, and probably because it was at Bethany's expense, in which case they must hope for an epic response, which was better for the paycheck. Her reactions had become fewer and farther apart. She wondered if production was getting nervous and if advertising was dropping precariously low, as Bethany had refused interplay with less and less people and to physically shop in stores rarely.

Sometimes her closest friends recommended cars and products and services, usually to no avail, except to get exceedingly angry with Bethany when she wouldn't buy what they were selling, beneath a thin veneer of friendship. Whenever Bethany talked about someone at work, inevitably she would walk past that co-worker later day, sometimes within minutes of her conversation. The gossip column at her work was faster than the speed of light, and her co-workers were fueled with information to say to her and about her to see how she would react.

Bethany hoped that ratings for her show had been plummeting as she removed herself from most exercises, only being social when necessary or due to a sense of obligation. She hoped that meant that the producers were running out of ideas to keep the show going and she prayed it would end.

Bethany didn't want anyone's feedback so she seldom shared. Most people reacted nervously, negatively or adversely to her view of the world, how she treated it and what she did in it. Bethany was used to it, so she rarely tried to fit in and gave up seeking new friendships. She hoped... she knew her soul had a reason for the path it picked for her to live, even though

Bethany admitted to herself, it felt mostly ridiculous. She received so many signs that there was more to life than reality, and Bethany eagerly embraced each and every clue.

She found it interesting that each morning she seemed to forget that she was loved, and each day looked for new assurances from Spirit that there was more to life than what she was experiencing now. If only she would remember to set every day the moment she woke up. Even the Producers couldn't have an effect when she connected to Spirit in the morning and agreed to align for the whole day. Miracle after miracle.

So Bethany attempted to get another job, and to extricate herself from most social get togethers and outings with the friends picked for her that day. The isolation from friends was slightly easier than the job hunt. Most of her TV co-workers and friends took the withdrawal personally and were offended, and either wanted to hurt her back or completely cut her out of their lives. Bethany understood their abandonment of her. It seemed a reasonable reaction to her escaping conversations with them and evading invitations to go out.

Her empathetic abilities had grown over the years and Bethany's antenna picked up a wide radius of everything. With the current state of affairs in the world, being around people was exhausting as most were angry, complaining, depressed or trying to justify why their lives weren't good and how they believed Bethany's life wasn't good as well.

Ascension and The Experiment

Bethany was in a bit of a spot. She had come to this planet to help in the ascension process, the experiment, and she had been wondering where the fuck the cavalry was. She had been waiting decades for the backup her intuition assured her had been promised, holding it together sometimes only by the hair of her chinny chin chin, waiting for the Good to arrive and to overcome the Fear. The advertising for this "adventure"

was phenomenal, and in hindsight complete bullshit. The "adventure" was wrapped in a big bow and looked like an amazing ride.

It called to those who could do – their specific purpose to emulate absolutely any culture and appear as one of the natives and give feedback on the status of the planet.

The catch - the feedback was to be presented in person, regardless of the current situation of the soul. Ergo, the Empath suicide pact. It seemed easy enough to agree to, come home when these conditions are met. Check. Add Signature. Check check. No problem. That's because when we are with Spirit, we can not know the pain of "individuality" and the duress of most of the human population. There is no way to feel less than complete love and adoration and fulfillment in the Vortex. The reference to Vortex from Abraham-Hicks teachings.

So the Experiment seemed an easy thing to accomplish when with Spirit. And those that reported, left the planet when supposed to, upon reconnection with Spirit, had no way to communicate the hardship associated with being human. Once they transitioned, those who were sent to monitor the conditions on Earth, quickly assimilated back to love and didn't have the capacity to express the weight of being human. Once back in the light, life was beautiful and magnanimous.

When the conditions were met, those that could do were required to report home, i.e. immediately in some cases. It sounded simple enough in the presentation until one was actually exposed to life on Earth. Living on the planet was difficult at best, to say the least, and agreeing to be human, and forget one's origin was far more complicated then the Organizers could discern from their perspective.

The Organizers knew that the third attempt would be treacherous at best, but in an effort to save the beloved Gaia, our Earth, they did what they felt they had to do. Being one of those that could do, and wanting to do something heroic, and allowed to feel that human emotion in preparation to go, Bethany agreed to the requirements of the adventure. Even the one to erase all memories of all other lifetimes and the truth of Our existence, since that the was the state of the current human. That desire to feel heroic was addictive, and the Organizers knew it would be enough to get the experiment on its third run, and get the participants needed to try and make it work.

In her childish optimism, Bethany assumed she would remember All with ease despite the procedure. Those that could do were processed before they were sent to Earth by having all but two of the human twelve DNA strands provisionally pinched off. Bethany told herself at the time of recruitment that she would figure it out with two strands, please, no problem. Little could the Organizers or Bethany foresee that the adventure would end unbelievably well, even though it would look, for quite a bit, that it was going horribly wrong.

2017 was a year in history, where it looked like end hours were upon the Earth and everyone was wondering what to expect next. Bethany knew that Gaia would rise up and defend herself, and knew that it may look terrible, but it would be perfect. Bethany sent prayers to the whole planet as Gaia starting really stretching her muscles in self-defense. The Earth had taken enough shit from the inhabitants and was letting them know.

Hurricanes, earthquakes,
fires, volcanoes, disease
Please
Ease our situation,
We are on our knees

Life

Why, if live things sprout from her skin, did humans not realize that the planet is Alive. Life comes from life. The Adventure here was to realize and find respect for everything in and on the planet, all life. To find tolerance for all, to remember that All Life is Sacred. All Life is seeking to keep itself Alive, until it stops desiring life or is so in love with life, they're good, and they exit. And so is Gaia, our Earth. She is our

Heart outside of ourselves. She has taken enough poisons and toxins in three dimension reality and has forcefully moved herself to the Fourth Dimension.

Bethany knew her mission was to help Gaia ascend to the Fifth Dimension. Helping people to feel better was part of that process, but she was tired as fuck of trying to help lift people's emotions. Most people were so addicted to feeling bad, pain and suffering that they attacked anyone who tried to lighten their load.

There is no journey that leads to an end of suffering and pain. There is Only One path which has Love for All. So although Humans in the now fourth dimension experience got addicted to suffering and pain and depression and loss and upset and anger and jealousy and hurt and obsession and malice and darkness, they should know without a shadow of a doubt, that those will be replaced with joy, chivalry, clarity, fun, celebration, greatness, kindness, compassion, strength, empowerment, gratitude, friendship, mysteries, elegance, beauty, family, relaxation, parties, bounty, song, wine, wind, ease and abundance in All. Welcome alignment with Spirit, welcome Fifth Dimension.

Typically, the life span of those that could do was kept average in order to not draw attention to their ageless tendencies. Although, they almost always draw attention to themselves because of their innocence, immaturity, belief in goodness, and dog like tendencies. Which leads the empaths to get themselves defiled, ruined, maimed, humiliated, tortured, made fun of, be the subject of witch hunts, killed, etc. The attempts on their lives were numerous indeed.

What to do with the mob mentality of wanting to kill what they fear? Assume they are ignorant? People panic and then bow down and kiss the ass of the person they think is the most confident, who in reality is the most afraid and the most insistent upon getting confirmation from large groups of people. Add to that, everyone thinks they deserve trust but aren't willing to give it. One of the most aggressive players in the adventure didn't understand why Bethany got offended at the pokes, jabs, and baseball bat swings to the gut, since they would yell out from time to time "it's just a game".

Bethany knew firsthand what it was to be a jerk, and while it could feel good for a hot minute, it usually came with a weight that seemed eternal and grew with each offense, like the chain and locks worn by Marley.

Really, there was nothing to fear here or in the afterlife. When you go back to the truth of our real existence, reviewing and reliving the whole of your human life from all perspectives is a huge growth experience and the reward for having lived as human is a massive expanse to the ever-growing universe. Hopefully, you learned to make yourself happy first and foremost, however plenty of time to go back in time and remedy All that was.

But Maybe that was the problem, it felt like time was collapsing and perhaps the time to go back and fix one's errors was quickly dissolving. All That Is had truly turned up events on the Earth to get humans attention to find their paths **now**. It was fine if they didn't get it, they would just have to keep going in a place known to Catholics as Purgatory, but it would be much better than perceived life as it is now on Earth.

So Much Good Coming.

Relief

Reviewing her past, Bethany realized she needed to forgive herself. She had turned away from religion as it had served to punish her as an innocent child. She had seduced an elderly gentleman at the tender age of six and she had always thought herself guilty as self-charged and didn't she deserve to suffer the consequences?

Had Bethany deemed herself innocent as she truly was, she would have missed the massive creative growth she acquired in learning to navigate the lies and threats of adults to manipulate her. Bethany had created an image of herself as a very bad child, and in this moment, forgave herself for damning her little girl to a life of strife.

Domestic Life

Bethany was watching Big Brother again. She wondered how much of an impact she took watching it. She wasn't ready to show all her true colors so she didn't insist they didn't watch it. She had already insisted that she couldn't watch the news. She had had to get really upset to make it clear that she meant it. She wished she could have politely asked and he would have simply acquiesced. She wondered if the producers pushed for news exposure. They must, as it was such a sure-fire way to hate your life and everything associated with it. Toxic goo.

She hated how he ran the faucet at full blast for an incredibly long time, all that water running, running down the drain. WTF?!? Come on!! He would nag her about leaving the lights on, and then the leave the refrigerator open, the oven open, the front door open, and run the kitchen faucet on and on (not true) and run the shower for ten minutes before he got in (also not true) but enough so it got Bethany's goat.

His luxury with water and electricity drove Bethany nuts, but not as much as his giving her shit about leaving the lights on. Of course, Bethany didn't want to admit that she ran the water and let it flow as long as she pleased. It was annoying when she thought of phrase 'the pot calling the kettle black'. What was really annoying was his ease at stepping in and out of the Illusion. For a time Bethany was convinced he had an evil twin. Not evil really, just not really into her. Yep, just like the movie 'He's not that into you'. She hoped that it was just one of his personalities. He had informed her that she had about fifty personalities and he was good with forty of them. Bethany was good with that, as she liked four out of his five.

Predator and Clues

A very large predator bird had just swooped through Bethany's backyard. It startled her as she quickly stood up to watch it drop into a neighbor's backyard. She hoped the family pet was inside as the predator looked like it was about to pick up lunch. It had darker colors than the small blond and light red hawk feather she had found outside on the front yard only thirty minutes earlier. She knew it was no coincidence.

Days before Bethany had found a beautiful blue feather in the front yard as well. She knew these were gifts from the Spirit world. She been noticing for months, maybe it was years now, that the local grey and brown sparrows she had grown accustomed to watching had been sporting the most beautiful blue and red tones. Like the red robin and blue bird of happiness had begun to show their true colors. Her beloved dog huffed a few times as Bethany rolled these thoughts around in her mind. He huffed a few more times as he went inside the house to scrunch up and lay on his sheepskin rug. She had found it at a garage sale while being on a thc induced high. On that same day, Bethany had also picked up a crystal decanter, a calculus book, Carl Sagan's Cosmos – hard copy and something else. She knew the item was important but it refused to reveal itself. …….ahhh, there it was – a bumper sticker that read "I am radioactive".

The powers that were had taken one of the most important words in the Illusion and had made it stand for something bad.

In her search for a dictionary to see how **radioactive** had been defined, as she remembered more of the items she had rescued from the garage sale, gifts from Spirit. In the middle of that train of thought, she wondered if her man wanted to fool around. She had felt more than seen a shimmer of a rainbow to her left, and felt her lady parts tingle in anticipation. She wondered if she should follow her urge to encourage that tingle, when the resident hummingbird in her backyard started to twitter a staccato sound of "titch, titch – get back to writing, stay the course".

Encyclopedia

Annoyed, but obeying, Bethany continued. Although her lady parts teased, she got up and found her Illustrated Encyclopedic Dictionary underneath the sparkly black pipe cleaner cob web that she had stuffed on top of the dictionary as a result of her forgetting to pack it away with the other Halloween decorations. She loved this large heavy book, and had used it frequently with her son in doing his elementary school homework but hadn't used it in probably fifteen years as the internet had pulled a large percentage of the populace away from paper.

Gardening

As she opened the very large and heavy book to look up the definition of radioactive, her eyes alighted upon the picture of a Hairstreak butterfly. Bethany had presumed it was a moth when she had seen it only hours earlier that day. A most beautiful deep orange color on its outer appearing wings as the back of both wings touched their color matched the orange poppy it had been perched upon. Bethany was so happy to see it, especially on the beautiful California poppies that she had finally successfully coached to grow in her backyard. She knew that the fairies had helped this to occur.

The Fae had been instrumental in this last awakening. They had probably been responsible for every awakening on Earth, but Bethany hadn't thought about giving them credit until the last decade or so.

The sight of her toes upon the comfy cushion of the deck furniture gave her pause. She had her reading glasses on, and she saw what she had missed yesterday, ambling most of her Friday at work in flip flops. She had long dark brown scraggly hair streaming from her big toes and monkey toes. She had been lazy in the shower and had shaved her toes cause they had been in a similar predicament a month, or so ago. Geez, how fast did the hair on her toes grow? Sometimes, reality showed up in weird ways, and Bethany knew she didn't enjoy this version.

She saw the limp fruit fly in her port she had poured hours earlier. Bethany attempted to save it using her pen, but it had already passed and she noticed the ink from the pen making a windy journey in her port. She cleared the energy that criticized her for putting toxins in her drink and got back to the clues at hand.

In her continuing search for the definition of radioactive, the book had opened to Hairstreak butterflies, and one had shown up earlier in the day. When the butterfly slowly and purposefully opened its wings, the inside colors were a beautiful green hue, with black etching on the outer rim encased in deep orange. Bethany knew it was a sign from Heaven that she was indeed, progressing on her path, and that help was on its way.

The hummingbird dictated a myriad of orders, emphasizing RIGHT NOW, that help is indeed here, although Bethany mostly heard terse commands and criticism of her procrastination. It felt like there had been delay after delay to the Ascension process. Her frequency shifted a bit at her old habit of criticizing herself and her progress. In truth, Bethany knew that only words of love and encouragement came from the hummingbirds, and from all life. If only Bethany would quit judging from a human standard - what was good and what was bad. It just was. Nothing was good or bad unless the ego allowed itself vanity and believed that it was above judgement but continued to judge all. Judging versus enjoying the Experience of trusting All.

Bethany's frequency dropped when she wondered what was taking her so long. So she paused for a moment to take in the beauty of it All. She loved the Ed Sheeran song, I'm in Love with Your Body. Bethany was in love with Gaia's body. She couldn't wait until she manifested enough Good to help Earth clean herself and feel better.

Indeed, Gaia is breathtaking.

Gaia

Bethany dreamed of swimming in her waters daily. That was the goal anyway, after following her gut instinct to set everything in motion to save her Heart. Freeing her Heart would mean Bethany assisted in liberating Earth, as a tiny Groot in the immense universal force to emancipate the planet from those who would decimate at will. Help beyond her wildest dreams.

She needed...she didn't need to, but she would like to listen to Ester Hicks again. The woman channeling Abraham was amazing, and Bethany was in awe of her. What a Phenom. And Mediums were making a comeback!!! John Edwards had kicked it off. Bethany knew she had found the real deal when she met John. He was giving a small workshop on how to meditate in Long Island after...or before doing readings for most of the attendees.

Bethany adored John and was fascinated with the gifted psychic medium, attending several of his events after the original meeting. Sometimes when he channeled, she sensed that he felt the heaviness of the emotions associated with communicating with families' loved ones, feeling their grief and pain of loss of those whom they missed desperately. She knew she had the gift but told herself it wasn't real and that she couldn't do it. What she needed was to create a lexicon to communicate with Spirit, but she had been reluctant. The obligation to give messages, with the motto – don't shoot the messenger – out in the world, seemed like a no win proposition.

Bethany had found Edward Cayce's book years earlier searching for answers. She had felt so much like Edward, and yet didn't have any interest in putting a Catholic spin on any of the information she received, nor did she care for the pain and suffering Edward Cayce seemed to endure. Yikes! There had to be a better way. And yet thank God for her being introduced to his work by a friend, who knew Bethany was intuitive, understanding, and compassionate enough to be free of judgment of another's experiences. The friend had been an abductee of aliens, the bad ones Bethany assumed as it was not a pleasant experience.

Her friend knew what it was like to experience scorn and derision for her truth. And Bethany understood not wanting to reveal this intimate and life altering event.

Bethany could feel that the abduction was real, and felt love for her bonded her with those that also been taken and returned. She hoped that the event had bonded her friend with the friends that had also been taken and returned. She had confided in Bethany because she could feel that Bethany was intuitive and understanding, and so trusted her with this deep dark secret. Bethany empathized with her. Being different hadn't been easy for those that could do.

She knew the Warriors for Earth (WE) – those that could do – were supposed to report Home when the frequencies became unbearable and caused those that could do to self-destruct in order to exit the program. The auto destruct mechanism kicked in and WE went home to report the conditions in person, so the Organizers could adequately staff and advise the new arrivals prior to their jump to Earth.

Bethany had disobeyed the self-destruct order too many times to count. She had stubbornly refused to kill herself, although, she had felt like she had received orders to do so since she was six. In the Human Gaia Experiment, Bethany had lost touch with her true origin and what was expected of her. She had tuned it to human beliefs that said going home was wrong and against the law. In the Illusion she was already a bad person for seducing an elderly gentleman, how mad was God gonna be when she showed up to see him at her own hands? Especially being raised in the Catholic Church.

And she had hated the Catholics for their beliefs, as she had been raised, as Bethany had always felt that everybody on the planet should be allowed to come and go as they pleased. Why make it wrong? So many Humans wanting to leave the Experiment, kept here by false guilt and lies. So many dutiful Warriors for Earth obeying their commands being painted as bad, as villians, as going to Hell? Please. Enough with the damning and bullying bullshit.

If Bethany heard another word about Hell she felt she might light something on fire, ironically enough. Probably herself. She had convinced herself at a very young age after seeing the movie Rosemary's baby, she was spawn of the devil. It didn't help that she had been exposed to The Exorcist as well. And it totally sucked to believe oneself evil when all you really wanted to be was Good.

Hyrax

Humans of Earth - believe in something else, believe in something better, something sweeter, something safer, something more beautiful than what you see now. Bethany understood there is almost a total population addiction to fear and negativity, but Search for the Light in Everything.

Bethany shifted her frequency and lightened up. Search for the Light in Everything.

The Illustrated Encyclopedic Dictionary revealed many clues to Bethany. As she reopened the book, she landed in the following places: Thoth (ⲧ)- "In ancient Egypt, Thoth - was the scribe of the gods, the inventor of numbers, and the measurer of time, from which Thoth became the god of wisdom and magic. Also the moon goddess and usually represented with the head of an Ibis." Bethany searched for ibis and was drawn to hyrax.

The caption under a picture of the hyrax read: Although hyraxes look like rodents, they have no close relatives. The nearest is thought to be the elephant. The animals, which grow between thirty and fifty centimeters (twelve to twenty inches) long, are native to Africa and southwestern Asia and have hooflike nails on most of their toes.

Bethany was curious about the last bit of the definition, which included the following: "more closely related to hoofed mammals (unicorns). Also called "dassie" and especially in the Old Testament "cony,"

New Latin, from Greek hurax *t*, shrew mouse." Hurax seemed very close to hyrax. Same word in the Old Testament?

Fairies

Anyone? Is this ringing a bell with anyone? Or is it more like an alarm going off? This isn't the world you think it is, it is so much more. Hidden for so long. It's time for all the Hidden to Come into View. How many fairy tales, myths, fables, tall tales ready to be exposed for the truths they contain.

Bethany knew she was tired of being mistreated because of her belief that free power existed and so did fairies, unicorns, talking animals, aliens – good and bad, and walking trees, and so much more. She knew that at her corporate job, they used terms to describe her, belittle her and call her a liar and a loser, but she knew that the truth would come out eventually.

Next, Bethany's eyes were drawn to hyssop, which seemed to jump off the page. She once read in the bible or was told in Catholic school that hyssop was offered to Jesus as he was on the cross. A woody plant, *Hyssopus officinalis*, native to Asia, having spikes of small blue flowers and aromatic leaves used in perfumery and as a condiment. Any of several similar or related plants. And unidentified plant mentioned in the Bible as the source of twigs used for sprinkling in certain Hebraic purifactory rites. Hyssop had legs back to Middle English, back to Old English and Old French – ysope – both from Latin, from Greek, and from Semitic, akin to Hebrew 'ezõbh'.

Then Bethany focused on looking up Ibis – Any of various long billed, mainly tropical, wading birds of the family Threskiornith-idae. It made Bethany think of Egypt rather than Florida. Next, her eyes were drawn to Ibiza – The third largest of the Balearic Islands; in the Mediterranean Sea, and the one nearest the lost coast of Spain. Ibiza is also the name of the largest town. Well, it was certainly a popular name in 2017 as it was referred to in a top forty pop song. Wasn't it in the song about the tiny bikini? Wait, Bethany had always thought Ibiza was in Brazil, not Spain. Did the Ibis originate in Ibiza? What was the connection?

Next, Bethany landed on a page that had lots of pictures, one of the very pictures featured on the cover of the *Illustrated Encyclopedic Dictionary*, which must be trying to get her attention.

For what? Where were all the clues supposed to lead her? Was she just on a wild goose chase? Bethany knew she ought to research each one, but it was getting cold outside and she was ready to go inside the house. Determined to note the last of the clues she had found in the moment, she documented *Radio Revelation* — as WE on Earth observe it at right angles to the disk shaped galaxy, the Milky Way. Huh?

Was the definition in the dictionary related to the Experiment?

She also noted that previously referred to Calculus book she picked up at the garage sale was actually an Algebra Two course book, and with it she had picked up a Simplified Electrical Wiring Handbook, The Great Radio Heroes by Jim Harmon in paperback, and The Bluejackets' Manual hard copy dated 1944. Bethany didn't think there was a paperback version of the manual from the United States Naval Institute, Annapolis, MD. And finally, the last thing she remembered that she picked up at the garage sale was the sheet music of the song "I Love You California" words by F. B Silverwood and Music by A.F. Frankenstein, no less. And Bethany did love California.

The setting sun interacted with Bethany via a sparkling presence and cheered her immensely as it reflected off a sparkly glass decoration in the backyard. She recited her evening prayer:

Hail to the Watchtowers of the West, Blue and Gold Sparkling Water, Archangel Gabrielle, Evening.

Ability to Go Home

Bethany smiled as she worked in the backyard the next day. She acknowledged All the plants growing, and they had a lovely energy. Bethany had learned to not take it personal when they left, or to make herself bad when she sent parts of them home either. Hadn't she always supported being able to go home when One wanted to?

Bethany had taken the dog out and as she strolled along couldn't hold her train of thought. She noticed a dark blue feather on the ground in front of her on this evening walk. The signs were multiplying – Good Is Coming, Good Is Coming – Spirit chanted it even as the Illusion beckoned at her with thoughts of grey cubicle walls and back stabbing co-workers and bosses.

After the walk Bethany went back to the backyard to sit on the deck and hang out. It was a beautiful warm. It was a beautiful warm summer evening, so much so that as her dog wandered around the backyard, sometimes it would lay down mid amble to soak up the heat still left in the concrete.

Decisions, decisions, go back in the house and lay on the sheepskin rug or hang outside and soak in the Sun? Unable to decide, her dog sauntered and chewed on grass growing through cracks between the house and the foundation. They had stopped using weed killer because they realized they were poisoning the dog every time he chewed on a random piece of grass when they had used it before. So judgmental - those weeds, so not good enough.

A little Alice in Wonderland, or was it Alice through the Looking Glass? Bethany had asked the HOA "gardeners" to stop using pesticides on her lawn, but she didn't know if they honored her request. Most of the landscapers seemed like they worked for Hitler the way the butchered the plants with weed wackers, spread poison to avoid bending down and pulling out weeds, and used those infernal blowers loud as fuck to blow grass cuttings and leaves into the homes of the HOA one street down. Bethany knew the day would come when people took responsibility for their trash.

And then she asked herself to change the subject.

She had been listening to a lot of Abraham channeled by Esther Hicks and it was enlightening. Listening to Esther allowing Abraham to come through her and give messages felt liberating and empowering to Bethany. The messages entertain freedom, the freedom that every life form is entitled to. Bethany thought it would be nice to behave as one would wish while following the Golden Rule – Do unto others as you would have others do unto you.

Bethany saw two flashes of almost hot pink color reflect off her laptop. Hot pink but deeper. She had learned these were signs from Archangels.

Bethany saw an article about Paws On The Ground and it announced that the Cavalry had arrived. Thank God!!!! It was the news Bethany needed. It was the news the world needed to hear and be able to believe. People were so weary.

There had been so many signs of the Good Coming, but they had been coming more often and more impactful this last year.

And all the ones in 2018 had sounded stronger than the previous years. She knew that others may not be able to see it yet, but she had faith enough for herself, and for others. Somehow Bethany had been blessed to have faith in the unseen and not care whether there was accord. She did prefer situations where she was able to feel understood and it was lovely to get confirmation. But she had learned from Esther, channeling Abraham, that it was incredibly powerful to feel better by choosing thoughts that allowed relief, rather than relying or depending on others to get it.

Bethany looked forward to experiencing all the good she had imagined for and all those she loved. She had always believed in happy endings, loved Disney and Hallmark, dreamed of a world gone well, with joy to All, and with Love for All.

If she wanted to feel better, she could focus on things that made her feel good or imagine her life the way she had dreamed about. The whole point of the movie *Tomorrowland* - which wolf you gonna feed?

The Good Witch

Bethany had been bending time again. She had started moving through time twenty years ago or so and had begun to master it when her world had been turned upside down. It had been a long time since she had been easy in her life and able to move through time. She had suspected it for weeks, as she spotted the anomalies in her departure and arrival times in her day to day. It was a lovely tool to have more time. Thank God for Louise Hay. "I take my time as I have all the time I need." This simple statement had helped Bethany feel like the witch / fairy / water sprite / alien / goddess she knew she was.

She determined that she be less obvious in case she frighten the villagers. It took the locals quite a while to figure out that she had no interest in them if they left her alone or interacted kindly with her. She had scared people in her past lives and the frightened villagers would get together and try to light her up. Hadn't she been torched enough in past lives, and didn't she want to forget?

Forgiveness

Bethany was glad it was a new moon. It was time to usher in change, how simple. The greatest magic of all was to love oneself. For a lot of us that means forgive oneself. The Catholic Church wrapped forgiveness in a bow, and gave it out like a present at Christmas, only on special occasions and only after pleading for it to a man. Although it was more of an Easter thing really. But ye be a blasphemer that thinks Ye can forgive yourself without a priest.

Arg!! Pirates they be, those Catholics. How dare they ban the key to ascending. The key, held in clues in the papal lands, concealed in allowed scripture, and hidden away with our loved ones who pass over.

Bethany felt that her angels must be exhausted. She had pushed most limits she was exposed to, even though she knew she appeared to be a rebel without a cause. But Bethany had gotten the final sign to complete her work. This was it, the life she had been living was that of Truman, and she knew it was about to end. The feeling washed over her body in a silvery way, sweeping along her spinal cord and winding up to her brain stem in what felt like peppermint warming and cooling the path to her head from her tailbone. And as her Soul had told her definitively before, she would miss the heart connections she had made, but as her elation grew Bethany felt joy and eagerness in looking forward and finding the Good.

Inspirations and Recommendations:

* Esther and Jerry Hicks - Abraham Hicks teachings

* Anything by Louise Hay

* The Holographic Universe by Michael Talbot

* The Journey Home - A Kryon Parable

* Conversations with God - John Walsh

* Let's Pretend This Never Happened - Jenny Lawson

* Early work Oracle Cards - Doreen Virtue

* John Edward - Psychic Medium

* Teresa Caputo - Long Island Medium

* Henry Tyler - Hollywood Medium

All those clues from Spirit, especially radioactive. Probably our true nature - radios picking up on signals being flowed into our world. Surely there must be a special understanding that Bethany was being led to gain. She would have to connect these signposts from her Guides to figure it out, but where, oh where, were the clues leading her next?

About the Author

The author pens from her heart and asks that all who read her writings seek to move the 'h' from the end of our beautiful planet's name to the beginning - and love their Heart.

Lastly, and maybe most importantly, I want to thank my best friend JB, whom without none of this would have come together.

9 781956 529449